MW01133766

DEADLY INTENT

Strong Women, Extraordinary Situations

Book Two

Margaret Daley

Deadly Intent
Copyright © 2014 Margaret Daley

http://www.margaretdaley.com/

ONE

.

Texas Ranger Sarah Osborn approached the man at the paddock. He faced away from her, his arms resting on the top slat of the fence. His tall, lean build radiated tension as he fisted his hands. She could see his biceps flexing beneath the T-shirt. There'd been a time she knew Ian O'Leary well. But not anymore. Maybe never.

"Ian," she called out. "I'm here about your stolen stallion."

He stiffened, pushed away from the wooden railing, and swung around. The tan cowboy hat shadowed his expression, but there was no mistaking his anger—the hard line of his jaw gave that away. "I heard you were assigned to this area, but I'd expected the sheriff. What's a Ranger doing investigating a stolen horse?"

"I'm heading a multi-county investigation into the recent cattle rustling."

"My prize stallion was taken. I don't have many cattle on this ranch, but the ones I have are accounted for."

"Sheriff Denison and I thought since a few horses have been taken, too, that this is the work of the same cattle rustlers." She didn't have to see his dark blue eyes to know they were drilling into her.

"Very well. What do you need from me?" A tic twitched in his cheek.

"To tell me what happened."

"I went through this with the sheriff this morning on the phone."

"Humor me. Run through it again." She ground her teeth to keep from saying what was really on her mind: *Why did you come home?* Since she worked several counties in this part of northeastern Texas, she'd managed for the past six months to keep her distance, but she couldn't avoid him forever.

2

He turned to the fence and gestured with his hand. "I keep Thunder near the barn. This is his paddock."

"When did you notice him gone?"

"About six this morning. I walk by here a bunch of times every day, since my home is so close."

As she walked toward the fence, she glanced over her shoulders at the simple red brick, one-story house with a long front porch, and if she remembered correctly from when they'd dated fifteen years before, it had a deck off the back that over-looked a large pond. "I heard about your father. I'd have been at the funeral, but I was on vacation when it happened. I didn't find out until I came home a week after-wards."

"He went fast and didn't suffer much. I didn't get to say good-bye..." Ian swallowed hard.

She fixed her gaze on the lower half of his face, the only part she could see. For a few seconds his lips, frowning, drew her to-tal attention. Memories of that mouth kiss-ing her flooded her mind, and her heart

3

rate accelerated. "I'm sorry. He was a good man."

"The best."

"The last I heard you were working in Houston for the FBI. What made you come home now and run the ranch?" Now, when it was too late for them? Now, when her heart had finally scarred over where he'd broken it in two. And why did she care, anyway? It had been fifteen years.

"I promised my dad I wouldn't sell the ranch. It seemed appropriate I carry on for him."

"He had the best rodeo horses in this part of Texas, maybe in the whole state."

"Which may be a reason someone took Thunder. He's sired many champions."

Thunder, his stallion. That's why she was here at the Shamrock Ranch. She had to find out what she needed and leave. "When was the last time you saw him?"

"Last night about eleven."

"You were at the barn late?"

"No, looking out my office window. It gives me a good view of Thunder, the barn, and some of the fields where the mares are. There's a security light that shines on the barnyard and into the front of the paddock. He was at the fence."

"So he was taken between eleven and six. Did anything unusual happen in the middle of the night? Did you hear anything out of the ordinary?"

"Frisky barked"—he paused and tilted his head—"about two this morning. But Dad's dog does that most nights. I tune him out unless he persists. He didn't."

"Where's Frisky?"

Ian scowled. "At the vet's. Whoever took Thunder poisoned him. Doc Miller is keeping him overnight, but he should recover."

Sarah started for the gate into the paddock. "I'm going to take a look around."

"I already have. There are boot prints. There was only one set I couldn't rule out—size twelve or thirteen."

"One person? Are you sure?"

Finally Ian pushed his hat's brim up his forehead so she could clearly see his expression. "I might have left the FBI, but I've been a law enforcement officer at least two years longer than you. Also, I'm usually the only one who handles Thunder. It took me several months to come to a truce with the stallion."

"Temperamental?"

He nodded, removing his cowboy hat and raking his fingers through his thick brown hair. "Until he accepted me, my dad was the only one who dealt with him. That's why I'm surprised someone snuck into his pasture, grabbed him, and got away without Thunder making a lot of ruckus."

"If they poisoned Frisky, maybe they did something to Thunder to make him more docile."

"I suppose the person could have tranquilized him." Ian pointed to the boot prints near the railing by the gate. "As you can see, a truck pulling a trailer was backed up to this area."

"No ransom demand yet?"

"I wish. Then I would know Thunder might be returned. I haven't heard anything. If he isn't found, it will set the ranch back financially."

"Does anyone hold a grudge against you?" *Besides me*. But even she didn't, not really when she thought about why they'd parted years ago. She couldn't fulfill his dream of being in the FBI and making a difference, especially in keeping this country safe from terrorists. His best friend had died in a terrorist attack, an attack that haunted Ian. He was supposed to be at the courthouse in Dallas that day. But he'd been delayed.

After that, Ian was driven to stop terrorists from attacking innocent people. And in the process, he'd probably earned himself an enemy or two.

"I've put my fair share behind bars, but most of them are still in prison."

Sarah used her cell to snap some pictures of anything that might be evidence, but she had to agree with Ian. There wasn't much to go on. After she made a cast of the shoe print Ian had indicated didn't belong, her gaze connected with his. He had a way of looking at a person and making her feel possessed by him, as though he could read her mind.

She blinked and looked at his hat, his T-shirt, the ground, until she got her bearings back. Only then did she peer at his face again. "So no other horses or cattle are missing, just Thunder?"

One corner of his mouth hiked up. "That's what I said. If I remember anything else, I'll let you know."

"Please do. If it's the cattle-rustling group, stealing Thunder may mean they're branching out. He isn't an ordinary horse, but a prize stallion." She dug into the pocket of her tan pants and pulled out a business card, then wrote her cell number on the back of it. "It's easier to get ahold of me through my cell phone. I'm not in the office much. I have several counties to cover, so I'm on the road a lot. If they contact you about a ransom demand, please let me know. Do you have a photo of Thunder?"

"Come up to the house. I have one in my office. Thunder has a microchip injected in him to help identify him, so even if they change his outer appearance, we'll know when we've got him. But the scanner used to ID the horse has to be close to pick up the signal. No GPS tracking yet." Ian shut the gate and walked toward his house. "I've contacted the Equine Protection Registry, and he was put on their Hot List, which goes out to various agencies. The microchip can't be removed without surgery."

"Too bad about the GPS."

"Yeah, I know. One day that will be available, but that doesn't help me now. I had a tag with a GPS tracking system on Thunder, but I found it by the gate, smashed. If they try to take Thunder out of the country through legal channels, I might get him back. But I think he'll stay in the U.S. The rodeo circuit is strong, and a good horse is valuable."

"Some ranchers have microchips in their cattle. Our modern day branding. But there is a black market for cattle. A person can make good money with the price of beef so high." Sarah studied the tire tracks leading away from the gate. "How many people do you have working for you?"

"Two hands that have been with the ranch for years—Charlie and Tony. They aren't involved."

"Charlie was here when you and I..." For some reason the word *dated* wouldn't get past the lump lodged in her throat.

A few seconds passed before Ian said, "Yeah. Tony was hired five years ago. There were other cowhands, but they haven't been here since Dad cut back on the number of cattle last year." Ian opened the back door and waited for her to go inside first.

Stepping into the kitchen, she felt as if she'd stepped back in time. She and Ian would come in after riding and grab something cold to drink. Her gaze strayed to the same oak table in the alcove where she would sit with Ian right next to her and dream of the future. The memory sent her pulse rate up a notch.

Ian gestured toward the office down the hall, the same one his dad used for years. "Make yourself comfortable. I won't be long."

As she made her way toward the office, she could feel Ian's stare on her, but there was no way she would look back to see if she was correct. She hadn't been enough for him all those years ago. She'd been finishing her senior year in high school when he'd left the small junior college nearby. She'd been planning on going to school with him, but he'd been driven to seek his own path—without her.

Inside the office she strolled around, taking in what was new and what was old. A photo of him on his horse graced the wall behind the large desk. There was a time he'd thought that horse would be his partner on the rodeo circuit. That had been important to him once, but he'd discarded that dream, too. She paused at the window and glanced out, noting Thunder's paddock and the barn, just like he'd said.

Why had Ian come home now, after all this time? He promised his dad he would run the ranch, but the Ian she had known wouldn't have given up on his dreams for anyone. He sure hadn't given them up for her. Why did he leave the FBI for his father after his death? And why now?

Ian cupped his hands under the flowing water and rinsed his face. Looking up, he caught his reflection in the bathroom mirror. He was the same man who had come home months ago, after leaving his *dream* job to run the family ranch. And yet, he wasn't that man. He certainly wasn't the same naïve kid, filled with purpose, who left fifteen years ago to do his duty, to avenge his friend's death. He'd wanted to rid the world of terrorists, but for every one he'd put away, two were there to take his place.

In the past years, he'd thrown himself into his job in the counter-terrorism unit and had rarely visited home. Now, his dad was dead. Had he ever told him how much he loved and admired him for his integrity and faith? He should have told him. He should have spent more time with him, especially the past year of his life. His dad had been more tired than usual, not his normal self. But when Dad had assured him he was fine, Ian had wanted to believe that was the truth. He should have insisted his dad go to the doctor.

He should have been with Brandon when that building exploded. His best friend had been there because of him. He'd talked Brandon into also applying for a summer internship.

One more mistake to add to his list. Even after all these years, guilt still weighed his shoulders down. His gaze dropped away from his image, and he concentrated on drying his hands.

As he walked toward his office, he composed his features into a neutral expression, determined not to reveal how much Sarah's appearance had shaken him today. He knew when he'd returned to Blue Creek that he might see her, but he'd expected the sheriff this morning. He'd had no time to ready himself for all of the memories. Sarah reminded him of the things he'd left behind when he took off all those years ago, full of anger and guilt that he had survived while Brandon hadn't.

Ian paused in the entrance to the room, his gaze fixing on Sarah, who was looking out the window. Her coffee-colored hair grazed the top of her shoulders in soft waves. He remembered when it was even longer, when he'd run his fingers through it.

She turned, her big green eyes locking with his. For a few seconds he forgot to breathe as memories deluged him—feeling lost in her beauty, the touch of her lips against his, the sensations she ignited in him.

Was she the reason he'd never married? No, he couldn't blame it on her. He'd thrown his whole life into his job, and now he had little to show for it.

She broke away from his stare and pointed outside. "You have a nice view from here. What time did you leave the office last night?"

"Midnight."

"Did you go right to bed?"

Transfixed by the hint of red coloring in her cheeks, he didn't answer right away. When one of her eyebrows rose, he finally said, "Not long after that."

"So the thief must've come after that, or I'm sure you would have noticed something. From your description of Thunder, it probably took at least twenty or thirty minutes to drug Frisky and get the horse into a trailer."

"I agree. Longer if the culprit didn't do

something to subdue Thunder."

"Where is your bedroom in relationship to the barn?"

He frowned. "The other side of the house in the back, so I wouldn't have heard a vehicle go by. I sleep pretty soundly." One of the perks of coming back to the ranch. He had fifteen years of restless nights to make up for.

"I wish..." She shook her head and swung around. "Do you have any surveillance cameras on the property?"

"Only one at the front gate, but I looked this morning, and it's been damaged. It had been working, so the thief disabled the camera before driving the horse trailer onto the ranch."

"Was it visible or hidden?"

"Hidden." He twisted his mouth into a scowl. "Which means the thief cased this property before taking Thunder. He knew about the camera and Frisky. And he'd have known about Thunder's irritable disposition, not that it was a secret, and brought something to help him get the stallion into a trailer without much noise."

She glanced over her shoulder. "Where's that picture of your stallion?"

He crossed to the desk, opened a drawer at the bottom, and pulled out a photo. "He's black as midnight with one patch of white running down his nose." Staring at the magnificent animal, Ian admired his sleek lines, the proud lift of his head, as he looked right at the camera. "Smart as a whip. It's his way or no way. Maybe I'll get lucky and the thief will return Thunder because he's too much trouble."

"If only life were that convenient." Sarah took the picture. "I'll get this out. This may or may not be connected to the cattle rustling, so I'll have the sheriff follow up on the theft. I probably won't return unless I discover that connection. You should keep an eye on your cattle, though."

"I've already brought them in closer to the barn. I'll have Tony checking on all the animals throughout the night. But that is only temporary, because I need him working days. If the cattle rustlers aren't caught soon, I'll have to hire someone for the night shift. I only have a little over a hundred head, but I don't want to lose them."

She started for the hallway. "You don't have to show me out. I know my way."

Ian followed her to the front door and onto the porch anyway. He glanced at the swing, just big enough for two. They'd spent many evenings sitting on that, talking, laughing…kissing. As she descended the steps, he almost asked her to stay a while and catch up. But he swallowed the words. She'd made it very clear from her tense body to her standoffish behavior that she wanted to get as far away from him as possible. And he couldn't blame her, not after what he'd done. What he wouldn't give to have those years back.

At one in the morning Ian fell into bed, exhausted. He'd spent the day contacting horse owners who'd had appointments to use Thunder's stud services for their mares. He'd spoken with a lot of disappointed folks today, but nobody could be as brokenhearted as he when it came to Thunder.

Fortunately, he was too tired to think about it any longer, and he fell asleep almost immediately.

Sarah, fresh and beautiful at only eighteen flittered through his dream. He held her hand and marveled at how perfectly it fit in his own. He thought of all they would do together, of the future they would have, the home, the children. Then the sound of an explosion, and he dropped her hand. She seemed to drift away from him, but no. It was he who drifted, leaving her standing in place.

Her smiling face disappeared, replaced by a young couple, the woman crying and the man helpless to do anything but pray.

Ian approached the house with his team to assess how best to proceed. Gunshots split the silence. One. Two. Then a long pause before a third discharge. Each sound shuddered down him. He gave the signal to rush the place, praying that the man and woman were still alive. He burst through the front door as other agents came in from the back. The sight of the couple on the couch next to each other, their feet and hands bound, their eyes staring at him. But what riveted his attention were the bullet holes in their chests, and the blood staining their clothes.

He panned the room. Where was the killer? As his team fanned out and searched the house, he tested a closed door. Locked. He motioned for the battering ram they'd brought. He pounded it against the wooden structure over and over until it crashed open...

A pounding sound continued echoing through Ian's head, followed by his phone ringing.

Ian. Pick up, filtered through his sleep-drenched mind.

Fumbling for his phone on the bedside table, he opened his eyes, darkness surrounding him. "Ian here."

"It's Tony. I'm at the back door. Let me in. There's a problem with the cattle in the west pasture."

"I'll be out in a second. Wake up Charlie." Ian hung up and rolled out of bed.

Three minutes later, he strode toward the cabin Tony and Charlie shared behind the barn. As he arrived, Charlie stumbled out of his place, buttoning his shirt. Tony was right behind him.

"What happened?"

The two men faced him, the light from the doorway behind them illuminating the area. Charlie looked as confused as Ian was, but Tony's expression told him enough.

Ian needed answers. "Are we missing cattle too?"

"I wish. This is worse. I found five cattle dead by the pond."

"How?"

"Don't know. When I was making my rounds, I saw them down, checked the nearest one, and couldn't see any cause."

"Let's go." He didn't know what to expect. "Charlie, bring your shotgun. I'm getting my weapon."

Ian hurried to his house, noticing the eastern sky reflect the grayness of predawn. He grabbed his loaded Magnum 45 and rushed back to his hired hands.

"We'll go on foot." Since the field was close, Ian didn't want to saddle a horse. By the time he did, they could be there. But he did quicken his step, scanning the terrain as he went. Tony had a powerful flashlight that lit their path.

As Ian climbed over the pasture fence, he saw the still bodies just a few feet from the water. He headed for the nearest one and used the flashlight to check the animal closely. No visible signs of how it had died.

Then he looked around, shining the light on the ground near the cattle, and then toward the edge of the pond. He grew rigid as he stared at the water. "I know what killed them."

TWO

For the second day in a row, Sarah pulled up to Ian's barn and parked. She made her way to the field behind the house. The sheriff called her that morning and asked her to come to the ranch again. Apparently, Sheriff Dan Denison and Ian were buddies. She'd asked him why he couldn't take care of it himself, since killing cattle was not the rustlers' mode of operation. What good were dead cattle? But he'd insisted.

She hadn't wanted to see Ian again, at least not until she could get her emotions under control. She should be angry with him. After all, he dumped her and moved to Austin to finish school at the University of Texas.

But she could remember her grandma telling her how important it was to forgive. God expected her to forgive. And she wanted to, she did. But it was easier said than done. She'd mourned his departure as though he'd died. And now, just like that, he was back in her life. She didn't know how to feel about that.

When she came to the fence, she assessed the crime scene. Five cattle lay on the ground, and Doc Miller was examining one of them. The rest of the cows had been moved to another pasture. But what chilled her in the warm spring air were the fish floating on top of the pond, most likely indicating a poison in the water. The rotten smell roiled her stomach, and that muffin she'd grabbed at the coffee shop threatened to come back up.

Ian crouched beside one of the dead animals. When he saw her, he stood and strode toward her. A fierce expression lined his tanned face. "Dan got called away to a break in. You didn't need to come. This has nothing to do with the cattle rustlers. They steal the cows; they don't kill them."

"I agree. So why did Dan want me on this case?"

"He thinks someone is after me."

She scanned the area. "He may be right. Who would want to hurt you?"

"I've put away lots of criminals over the years. So if someone's after me, I'll deal with it. I can take care of myself."

She didn't want to be here anymore than Ian wanted her to be, but the sheriff asked for her assistance. She couldn't ignore Dan's request. "Okay, we'll get to that list in a minute. Is there anyone else besides those criminals?"

Ian scratched the back of his head. "There is somebody. This man has been trying to buy the ranch. I think a criminal with a grudge would just come after me, but Peter Taylor ... he could have a reason to do this. He's been after this property for a long time. Dad wouldn't sell it, and neither will I, but about once a week he comes by and asks. He might be trying to get me to give up."

Sarah used her palm as a sunshield and scanned the horizon. This land had been in the O'Leary family for generations. She could see why Ian wouldn't want to sell it, but if he did, it would make her life easier. She wouldn't mind knowing she never had to look into the face of her lost dreams again. But this wasn't about her. "Why this property in particular?"

"He bought my neighbors' land on both sides of me a couple of years ago."

"Hmm. Well, if he's your culprit, then you're right. The sheriff could take care of this."

"True. I think he's so focused on the county fair this weekend. He and his men will be strained just keeping the peace there. That's probably why he wants you involved."

Probably. Which meant she was stuck with this case. "Where did you move the rest of the cattle?"

"To the east field. I'm hiring a few guards. I've been expanding the business, but this is going to set me back. Doc Miller will take some samples to discover what kind of poison was used. I don't want any residual effects from the poison in this field. It won't be used until everything checks out okay."

"Since most of your money comes from your horses, I'd be stabling the more valuable ones and posting a guard, at least at night until we find the culprit."

"I hate it, but I've already told Charlie and Tony to do that."

"After you're through cleaning this up, I need you to write down everyone you think could have done this. Start with your more recent cases and the convicts released from prison. In the meantime, I'll have a word with Mr. Taylor next door. I assume he lives on his ranch. Which one?"

"The one to the east."

"It's been a while since I've been out here and had a good look around. Do you mind if I borrow one of your horses? I'd like to get the lay of the land, so to speak."

"Sure. When you come back from talking to Taylor, I'll go with you. With everyone crawling all over this place, I doubt anyone is hanging around, and so far, he's only struck at night. But still, I'd prefer you not go alone."

"I'm not the target. You need to stay here where it's safe."

His gaze drilled into her. "I can take care of myself. I won't hole myself up in my house. I have a ranch to run."

Someone could be after Ian. Want him dead. As they stared at each other, she realized her feelings for Ian were still there, buried deep in her heart. She didn't want them to grow and take over her life as they had when she was a teenager. "Fine. I'll be back after lunch." She began to walk away, stopped, and turned back. "Have you thought this might not be connected to last night, that some chemical has leaked into the ground water? You should have your water tested and any other source of water you use."

"I'm already on it."

"Good. And when was the last time someone checked this field in daylight?"

"Tony came around seven last night. There were no dead fish in the water, and all the cattle were fine."

27

"When did he find the dead cattle?"

"At five-thirty. He checked back a couple of times during the night. The last time around three. As far as he could tell, the cows were fine."

"Good. Now all we have to find out is what the poison is." She tipped the brim of her cowboy hat and continued toward her Jeep.

She didn't tell Ian that she would be checking out Charlie and Tony as well as the others on the list he gave her. She couldn't rule anyone out. She'd heard through the grapevine that Charlie had offered to buy the Shamrock Ranch from Ian before he'd decided to return. Could one of Ian's trusted hands be the culprit?

As Ian finished saddling the second horse for Sarah, she pulled up in her Jeep and sauntered toward him, looking every bit a Texas Ranger, even without the tan slacks that went with the uniform. The silver star, pinned over her heart on her white shirt, glittered in the sunlight. A year ago, Sarah joined the ranks of the Texas Rangers, one of the few females to do so. When he'd heard from Dan about Sarah, he'd been impressed, but not surprised. There was no goal she couldn't accomplish if she set her mind to it.

"What did my neighbor have to say?" He handed her Sugar's reins.

"He couldn't believe I would even suspect him, which only heightens my suspicion."

Ian mounted a stallion. "He's driven, but I'm not sure he would resort to killing animals. He thinks if he throws enough money at a problem it will take care of it."

"Do you have the list?" After swinging into the saddle, Sarah nudged her horse forward.

"Yes. I left it on my desk. When we get back, I'll get it for you. I did some checking, and as I said, a lot of the people I put on that list are in prison. So you only have twenty-three to check out."

Sarah blew out a long breath. "You have made a few enemies. This may take a while."

"I'll help."

"It's not your job anymore. I'm on this case, per the sheriff's request."

"It's my life, though. I want to help." Ian leaned over and unlocked the gate to the east pasture.

Sarah rode into the field. "Have you hired guards yet?"

"They start tonight. The men come from a top-notch security agency. I know the owner."

"So he isn't one of the twenty-three on your list?"

Ian chuckled, and for the first time that day, he began to relax. "Should I have added you to that list?"

She grinned, a twinkle in her eyes. "Fifteen years ago, I'd have been at the top, but not anymore."

"That's good. I didn't handle our...situation well."

"I wanted to be there for you. I knew how close you were to Brandon. Like brothers."

"I couldn't see much of anything right after it happened. I was so angry. I was at the parking lot across the street when the bomb went off. It knocked me down. One moment I saw Brandon in front of the building. The next he was gone." He looked out over the pasture, but it wasn't the land he saw. "I'll never forget that day. He was at the federal building because I asked him to meet me there." The rage and sadness swamped him all over again. "I wanted to be part of the FBI that went after the men responsible, but I was still in college. I couldn't do anything but stand on the sidelines."

"Haven't you forgiven those guys?"

Surprised at her question, he gripped his reins tighter. "No. Have you forgiven me for leaving you?"

A long moment ticked extra slowly until she finally answered, "Yes, but not the same thing. You need to forgive those terrorists who killed your friend. Let the anger go. It will only poison you."

"Like the water today?"

"Yes."

"I don't know if I'll ever be able to. There's a big difference between me leaving you and terrorists killing all those people."

Slowing her horse's gait, she tilted her head and looked at him. "Hate in any form damages the person who hates."

"You sound like my dad. Every time I came home he pushed me to forgive."

"That was because he loved you." Sarah's eyes widened, as though she had confessed she still loved him. She straightened in her saddle and spurred her mare to a faster pace.

He contemplated her words. Did she still have feelings for him? The thought brought a smile to his lips. He still cared about her, but they were vastly different people now from the two lovesick teenagers they'd been so long ago. But in spite of that warning, hope festered deep inside him. He urged his stallion forward.

Sarah stared at the water flowing in the stream and wondered if it was contaminated, too. This was one of her favorite places on Ian's ranch. Shaded by large cottonwoods and oaks, the sound of the water moving over the rocks and an occasional bird chirping calmed her soul. The scent of grass and vegetation laced the air. Spring, when everything was renewed, was her favorite time of year.

She couldn't believe she'd implied she cared for--okay, loved--Ian as his dad had. *I can't go there again. What if something else happens and he leaves. Lord, give me the strength to resist him.*

She heard Ian dismount behind her and wished he were anywhere but here. Why had she come to this spot of all the places on the ranch? She should have headed to the barn now that the tour was over.

"I'm not sure if I'm disappointed or happy we didn't find anything." His deep, baritone voice rumbled only a few feet behind her.

"Did you feel it?"

"Feel what?"

"Someone watching us."

"When we were near the fence line on the west side of my property?"

She nodded, a shiver snaking down her

spine. "I couldn't see anyone. I guess it could be my imagination conjuring up a bad guy."

"Not if we both felt it. I started to say something, but thought I was reacting to what happened last night."

"We can't dismiss any gut feelings. I'm sure yours has saved you on cases before."

"Strange how similar you and I are. When I heard you were a highway patrol officer, I was surprised. You never indicated you wanted to go into law enforcement."

"At seventeen—eighteen—I didn't have any idea what I wanted to do, but then I went to college and became interested in criminal justice. Along the line, I decided I was going to be a Texas Ranger, even though I knew I would have to work twice as hard to get in than a man would."

"Doesn't surprise me that you did it. Remember when you learned to rope cattle? You didn't give up until you could do it in less time than the state record."

She laughed. "Lot of good that did me. I hardly use that skill now."

"You mean you don't rope the bad guys

when they're running."

"I prefer a good tackle."

His chuckles peppered the air. The lines at the corner of his eyes deepened, and the gleam in their depths drew her to him. They had shared so many good times before the world's ugliness intruded.

"I'd have shot them in the leg and saved my energy." His expression warmed the pit of her stomach.

"Sure. I believe that. You're by the book. You aren't a rebel."

"After Brandon was killed, I came close, but you're right. Besides, if I didn't follow the law, the criminal might get off on a technicality."

"The things we do for a conviction." She grinned, feeling almost as comfortable with Ian as she had when they dated.

Silence fell between them. Ian stepped closer, and Sarah allowed him into her personal space. His outdoorsy scent engulfed her as though he had embraced her. He dipped his head toward her.

Out of the corner of her eyes, she caught a movement on the other side of the stream. Something in the foliage glinted. The hair on her nape stood up. Suddenly her survival instinct kicked in. She drew her Glock and shoved Ian out of the way.

A blast echoed through the glade.

THREE

As Sarah pushed him to the side, Ian spied her going for her gun, and he withdrew his Magnum 45. He twisted and aimed toward the threat. A bullet whizzed by his head, and he returned fire, lunging toward Sarah to push her behind the near-by cottonwood. Sarah discharged her weapon at the same time the assailant shot another round.

The bullet sliced Ian's arm as he drove Sarah and himself to safety, using the large tree as their shield. He peeked around the trunk. Ignoring the sting radiating from his injury, Ian squeezed the trigger. Sarah did likewise with her Glock. This time, the shooter didn't respond.

She stood against the cottonwood, and he shielded her body with his, just in case someone doubled around behind them. He leaned closer and whispered into her ear, "Do you think we hit him?"

Tense, as if every muscle were locked in place, Sarah slanted a glance at him. "Don't know. I'm calling the sheriff." With her free hand, she dug into her pocket for her cell phone. After she told Dan what happened, she disconnected. "He's sending a couple of deputies."

"We can't just stand here. He might be circling us to get a better vantage point."

"Shh. Listen."

Other than the rippling sound of the stream and their heavy breathing, quiet greeted him.

Five minutes passed before Sarah poked her head out and scanned the bushes.

He hated that she was in danger because of him. He pulled her back behind the safety of the tree.

She didn't resist. "The only direction he

can go is backwards. The space on both sides of his hiding place is too revealing. I think he's gone."

"What if you're wrong?"

"I'm going to dart to that oak closer to the stream. This one isn't big enough for the both of us side by side."

"I'm fine."

She stared pointedly at his arm, and he followed her gaze. Blood oozed from the wound and dripped onto the ground. "Fine, are you?"

"I will be. It's a flesh wound." He looked back at her. "You saved my life. He would have hit me square in the chest if you hadn't pushed me."

"I'm here to protect you. Let me do my job." She peered around the trunk again. "It was in the line of duty. Your back was to him."

"My focus was on you."

She swiveled her head to look at him. "Not a good idea."

The feel of her brought back all the good times, the laughter, they'd once had. Their love. *Love that I walked away from*.

In the distance, sirens blared.

Sarah sighed.

"The cavalry will be here soon."

"Good. You need a doctor, and I need to check out the brush where the shooter was. If he was wounded and bleeding, he might have left a trail."

"You're going to leave me out of all the fun."

She gave him a narrow-eyed look. "Be serious." She checked again then twisted around until they faced each other. "Don't play the hero. Get medical help, or I'll turn this case over to Dan, overworked or not, and let him deal with you."

He bent forward, inches from her mouth. "You won't give up until you solve this. You're too much of a professional to do that."

She flattened her palms against his chest and pushed him back a step. "Don't press your luck, mister."

Now that the adrenaline from the shootout had drained away, the throbbing ache in his upper arm demanded his attention. He took the bandana from around his neck and tied it over the wound. "I'll seek help, but promise me you'll come back to-night so we can start working on the list of suspects. This has to end."

"I'll get the list when I leave."

He blew out a long breath. "I want to work on it with you. I told you—"

"I can manage it. It's my job."

"What are you really afraid of? That be-ing around me might make you remember what we had?"

She pushed him another step back. "You're the one who left."

"I was a twenty-year-old on a mission, not thinking of consequences."

"You thought I would wait patiently for you to come back?"

"No. I knew you wouldn't. I wasn't clearheaded then."

Both of her eyebrows hiked up. "And you are now? What do you want from me?"

That was the question, wasn't it? What did he want? He'd pursued his dreams and caught a lot of bad guys. Now he was back. He'd thought he was happy until she showed up the day before. Now, he realized there was a gaping hole in his heart, a hole shaped way too much like the woman in front of him. What did he want? He swallowed and spoke the truth. "A second chance. We've both changed, and it might not work—"

"Like before?"

He nodded, the pain in his arm intensifying. A little scratch shouldn't hurt this bad. He sure wasn't going to let on how much pain he was in. "We're too different to go back to the way it was. But I still care about you, and I think you care about me."

She dropped her gaze to his chest. "Of course I do. You're a human being. I've sworn to protect you."

She hadn't lost any of her stubbornness. That was okay. He was just as determined today as he was at twenty. "Please come back to my house later. You can have dinner with me. I need to go through the list with you, anyway. All I wrote down were their names, not why they would be after me. It might help you prioritize the suspects."

"You haven't?"

"A fresh set of eyes might bring the insight I need."

Sarah leaned to the right. "Two deputies are headed this way. I'm going to ask one of them to take you to the ER and stay with you. I'm going to process the crime scene. Then since we both need to eat, I'll fix you dinner and work on the list until you return. Okay?"

"You cook? You didn't use to."

"You mean when I was eighteen? I've grown up a little since then. Did you really learn to cook, or was that a ploy to get me to volunteer?"

"I was going to take a frozen dinner out of the freezer and put it in the oven. That's the extent of my cooking." He dug in his pocket and grabbed his key. "This is to my house."

When the two deputies arrived, Sarah took charge and before he knew it, he was back at the barn and being escorted to a patrol car. He slid into the front seat and rested his head on the cushion. The throbbing in his arm pulsated through his body. He closed his eyes as the deputy pulled away from the barn, the blood loss catching up with him.

None of that mattered, because Sarah still cared about him, and that was a start. Of what, he wasn't sure.

After finding T-bone steaks in Ian's freezer, Sarah decided to grill them out back. That with a salad and baked potatoes would make a nice meal. Not fancy, but she had enough history with Ian to know he'd like it.

As she ran to the store to get the ingredients, she berated herself for offering to do this. At least his input on the names would help and she'd done what she could until she talked to him about the people on the list. She hadn't ruled out his neighbor, but the shooting earlier seemed beyond a simple, "I want to buy your ranch." Seemed more personal—and more serious—than that. The first two incidents had made his life difficult. The shooting—that was a big difference. She wondered, though—had the assailant shot to kill? Even if she hadn't shoved Ian to the side, the bullet most likely would have hit him in the right shoulder, not the heart. It wasn't a kill shot. It seemed to her the man—or woman—was toying with Ian. Another reason his neighbor wasn't high on her list of suspects. Or for that matter, Charlie. He'd been with Ian's family for years and more like an uncle to Ian.

While the potatoes were baking, she fixed the salad then put it in the refrigerator. She would grill the steaks closer to mealtime. She glanced at the clock. Ian would be here soon.

She moved into his office to get some more work done and saw Frisky lying by Ian's desk. He stood and wagged his tail. She'd met the brown mutt earlier when Charlie had brought him back from the vet.

She knelt beside the dog and petted him. "I'm glad you're okay. I'm going to get whoever poisoned you."

Frisky barked and sat as she rose. His tail swept back and forth on the hardwood floor. "Ian is lucky to have you." She gave Frisky a scratch behind the ears. According to the vet, he'd be resting more than normal for a couple of days.

She needed a pet. Her dog had died last year, and she hadn't replaced her. It had seemed too soon, but enough time had passed now. And truth be known, she was lonely. Was that why she kept going over what happened between her and Ian all those years ago?

After picking up the list on Ian's desk, she planted herself at the window to watch for his return, then scanned the names. If she wrote down the people who might come after her, how many would be on the list?

The longer it took for Ian to come home, the more she thought about their past. She began to question the wisdom of working with him tonight—in his home, full of memories. When the assailant had shot at them, she'd been scared, not so much for herself but for Ian. There had even been a few seconds at the stream the idea he could die had chilled her.

Headlights pierced the darkness out the window. Ian was home. Relief fluttered through her stomach.

As the deputy drove through the gate and parked in front of the house, she resolved to get back on a more professional footing with Ian. That was the only way this was going to work. What if her fear for Ian had caused her to freeze and not return fire? She'd never been this emotionally involved with the victim.

She laid the list on the desk and hurried outside. "I was beginning to worry someone hijacked you two," she said as Ian climbed from the patrol car, his arm sporting a white bandage.

Ian smiled. "Just rush hour traffic in Blue Creek." He leaned into the vehicle. "Thanks for babysitting me, Bryan."

As the deputy drove away, Ian mounted the steps, tension about his mouth and in his eyes. "It's nice to be home. I hate being poked and prodded."

She harrumphed. "Tell me about this rush hour traffic in a town of four thousand."

"Well, all four thousand must have been on the streets at the same time." He quirked a grin and passed her to go inside.

She swiveled around and crossed her arms. "Where did you go?"

His grin faded. He looked for a moment like he might make up a story, but then crossed his arms to match her stance. "I had Bryan take me to see Peter Taylor."

"Why? I already had." Before he could answer, she lifted her hands, palms out. "You know what? Forget it." She stormed toward the office. "Quit playing hero, or I'm out of here."

"I don't think he did this, but I thought I would cover that base once and for all. I informed him in no uncertain terms that he would never receive my ranch. I shared with him that I made arrangements with my lawyer. If I should die, Taylor won't be able to buy the land, under any circumstances."

She reached his desk and twisted toward him. "You've got to take this seriously. I know you've been an FBI agent, but I'm the investigator on this case. Not you."

"You don't think I am serious about this? Do you have any idea what it's costing me to have the poisoned pond cleaned up? The guards? They start tonight, which is a good thing. I need some sleep."

"I can stay and guard you tonight." Those words slipped out of her mouth before she could take it back, but on her cases she liked to be totally in charge and in the know. She was afraid he would try to do too much himself because he had been an FBI agent. "I mean out in my Jeep. In case something goes wrong. You know, I want to be close. To catch the guy."

"Forget it. There's no way I'm letting you spend the night in your car. That guarantees I won't sleep."

She remained silent. She'd do what she had to do, and she didn't need his permission. "Did the ER doc give you something for the pain?"

He nodded. "But I don't like taking stuff that puts me out. I have some over-the-counter pain meds I'm going to try first. I might take one of the stronger pills before I go to bed."

"I'm going to put the steaks on so we can eat. Then we can dive into your list."

She needed some space to calm down. She wanted this case over with so she could put some distance between her and Ian while she fought the feelings stirring for him—feelings she thought had died years ago.

"Sounds good. I didn't eat lunch today, so I'm starved." After greeting Frisky, Ian snatched the paper with the names on it off his desk and sank onto the brown leather couch in his office.

When she walked into the hall, she thought of something to say to him and re-traced her steps. His eyes were closed, his head resting on the cushion while Frisky lay beside him. She sneaked out. She'd delay dinner to give him time to catch a catnap. Maybe before she left the house tonight, she'd see some color return to his cheeks. That wound was worse than he'd let on. It must've required a bunch of stitches.

She made her way to the barn to find Charlie. She planned to protect Ian without him knowing, but she needed Charlie's help.

She stopped near the paddock fence. She wasn't a bodyguard. When had Ian become so important to her?

Fact was, it didn't matter. After the shooting, she feared this would end badly for Ian.

Hours later after dinner, Ian blew out a frustrated breath. He'd given Sarah a quick background on each of the names, but they were no closer to narrowing the list down. "Now you see my dilemma. Twenty-three people who might want me dead. They could all be prime suspects."

"You were doing your job." Sarah sat cross-legged on the couch next to Ian and tapped the paper with her ballpoint pen. "Tell me more about Tim Downs and Jagger Burns. They are the most recently released from prison. I can't believe Burns is out of jail."

"Good behavior and ratting on someone higher up in the group. I imagine he's long gone from Texas. He made a few people mad. I can't locate him, so his name is on the list. He was one angry dude when I ar- rested him. We couldn't charge him for the murders, because we didn't have enough evidence, but I looked into that guy's eyes. He killed those three people." The memory of Burns' smug expression tightened his gut.

Sarah's mouth flattened into a thin line. Her hand clenched around her pen. "I hate seeing the bad ones play the system." She glanced at the paper in her lap. "What about Tim Downs?"

"The quiet type. Explodes out of nowhere. If we hadn't stopped him in the planning stage, I'm sure he would have gone on to murder hundreds. Again, nothing concrete, but I've been around enough criminals with hearts full of evil to know one when I'm in their presence. He's at the top of the list."

"So his eight years in prison may have fueled ideas of revenge?"

"It's possible, but we can't live our lives worried about that, or we'd never do our jobs."

"Years ago I gave worrying to the Lord, or I would have been questioning every move I made."

"Exactly." Ian bent forward and rubbed Frisky, who'd hardly left his side.

After he gave her more information on the rest of the names, Sarah sat back and sighed. "First thing tomorrow, I'll start researching the names on this list. Their whereabouts. Their current associates."

"I'll help."

"You have a ranch to run. Keep your animals safe. This is my job."

Irritated, Ian said, "It's *my* life."

Her gaze locked with his as though delving deep into his soul. "You're going to do it anyway, aren't you? You always were determined. Stubborn, even."

"Look who's talking."

She took the list and tore it in half. "Here, you take those names. I'll do these." She waved hers in the air. "We need to know where they've been for the past—"

"I know what to look for."

She snapped her mouth closed and narrowed her eyes. "I've heard doctors don't make good patients. In this case, I'm thinking ex-police officers don't make cooperating victims."

53

He tapped his chest. "I'm cooperating. I'm helping." A sharp pain shot up his arm, and he rubbed it gently. He was so tired. He sagged against the cushion, the past hour going through the names finally catching up with him—or more exactly the past. Exhaustion gripped every part of him and wouldn't let go.

Sarah folded the paper and stuffed it into her jeans' pocket. "We've eaten, your kitchen is clean, and we have a game plan. Now, it's time for me to leave. You need your sleep. We have a lot to do tomorrow."

Each time she said *we* the word sang through his body. Maybe she would stick around after this was over. He realized he wanted that. "I can't argue it." He pushed himself up straight then stood. The room spun, causing him to wobble. He paused until the dizziness passed. Probably lost too much blood. In the morning he'd be back to normal.

"You okay?"

He shrugged. "Just got up too fast."

She cocked her head to the side. "First gunshot wound?"

"Yup. How about you?"

"Never had the pleasure."

"Let's keep it that way." He looked down at her, breathing in the scent of wildflowers.

She uttered a short laugh. "I'm with you on that." She slipped her arm around his waist. "I'll walk you to your bedroom then lock up as I leave."

He almost protested. But then he saw the concern in her eyes and shut his mouth. Besides, he liked the feel of her this close.

"Where are you sleeping?"

"My old bedroom."

She headed that direction, her pace slow, but he was just fine with that. The longer he could stay beside her, the better. At his door, he stopped and turned toward her.

He cupped her face. "You're beautiful. I've missed you."

She grinned. "Have you taken your meds?"

Her soft cheeks against his work-roughened palms sent his pulse pounding like a stampede. "Yes, ma'am. About an hour ago."

"Good." Her gaze shifted to his bandaged arm. "I don't like seeing you hurt."

"Neither do I." The words came out too slowly, and his thoughts began to jumble together. Weariness pressed down on him, and his eyelids drooped.

"Do you need me to help you to bed?"

The question shot a bolt of alertness through his dazed mind for a few seconds. "As much as I would like that, I'm fine. I'll be as good as new tomorrow."

"I'm sure you will." She reached around him and opened his door. "I think I'll help you anyway."

He didn't want to take his eyes off her, so she guided him backwards toward his bed. He stumbled on something on the floor and fell backwards, taking her with him.

FOUR

Sarah tumbled onto Ian's bed, landing on top of him. Heat seared her cheeks at their close contact, and she immediately scrambled off him and stood. From the hallway light, she saw Ian's eyes were closed. She knelt next to him on the covers and put her hand on his chest. It rose and fell slowly.

After taking off his boots, she lifted his legs onto the bed, threw a blanket over him, and crossed to the doorway. She glanced at his dark outline stretched out, asleep but alive and well. It could have been different. If she hadn't reacted so fast...if he'd moved a few inches in the wrong direction... That bullet might have gone through his heart. She grabbed the door jamb and leaned into it as a wave of anxiety overwhelmed her like thick smoke.

She'd come so close to losing him.

She cared more than she wanted to.

She watched him breathe a few more moments while the apprehension cleared. With a sigh, she left the room and checked to make sure everything was locked up. She paused on the porch. All seemed well. She headed to the small cabin and only knocked once before the older man opened the door.

Charlie stepped outside. "I'm glad you're here, Sarah. Any leads on who's behind this?"

"Working on that. Did you set it up?"

"Yep." He placed the key in her palm. "There's a cot set up in the tack room for you. I hate you'll be sleeping on it, though. It ain't very comfortable."

"Something's happened around here the last two nights, and after those bullets flew this afternoon, I decided I need to be here in case something else happens."

Charlie pushed his hat back and scratched his head. "Ian would kill me if he knew I was helping you. I'll keep him away. He's usually awake and down here by seven."

"I'll be gone by then. Did you say anything to Tony?"

"Nope." He motioned locking his lips. "Tony's already snoring away. Me and you are the only ones who know you're here. All he knows is that I locked both the back and front entrances to the barn. The guards are patrolling the fields and watching over the animals, not in the barn."

"Where should I park my Jeep?"

"There's a cutout not far from the gate. I'd park there. I'll wait in front of the barn until you walk back. Two guards just made their rounds along the front of the place. You should have enough time until they come back."

Sarah smiled. "We're going to get whoever is doing this." *So I can go on with my life without worrying about Ian.*

Sarah drove her Jeep out the gates of the Shamrock Ranch and parked where

Charlie had indicated, behind some large bushes that hid her car from anyone going by on the road. When she returned to the barn, Charlie left her to get some sleep, and she locked the front double doors. The back ones were already secured.

She walked down the middle of the barn, checking each stall, petting some of the horses and opening anything where a person could hide. With all the activity to-day, someone could have snuck in here and hid until everyone settled down for the night. Everything appeared all right. In the tack room, she turned off the light, alt-hough there were some on in the main ar-ea. She moved the cot to the entrance, so she could keep an eye on the doors and the horses. After lying on the blanket Charlie had supplied, she placed her gun within reach and closed her eyes. Fortunately, she was a light sleeper.

Sarah woke every hour and made sure the animals were all right. She might've caught a few winks during the night, but just a few. No worries, though. She could go days without sleep if she had to.

When the sunlight streamed through the large windows, Sarah stood and stretched and thanked the Lord for an uneventful night. She checked her watch—six-fifteen. She crept out of the barn, locking the double doors behind her. After pocketing the extra key, she raced across the ranch road into the field that ran alongside the highway. She climbed over the black wooden fence and strode toward the cutoff. When she reached her Jeep, she halted.

All four tires were flat.

Frisky's cold nose nudged Ian awake. Groggy, he wondered how he ended up on the bed like this with a blanket over him and his boots off. The last thing he remembered was... *Ah, Sarah*.

He'd almost kissed her in the hallway. He wished he had, but with all the crazy stuff going on, it probably wasn't a good idea to start anything. He wasn't that safe to be around. What if that shooter yesterday had hurt Sarah? He'd never forgive himself. And he had enough memories of

61

his own shortcomings to last a lifetime.

The image of that young couple filled his mind. The blood spreading across the husband's plaid shirt. The way the wife's lifeless arms cradled her unborn child.

How many times had he gone over that day in his mind? Logically, he knew he'd done everything he could have. Sometimes, the rescuers failed. Sometimes, innocent people died. Funny how that didn't make him feel better.

Frisky barked, pulling Ian away from the memories. He had enough to deal with in the here and now. No time to dwell on the past.

God was in control. Another thing he understood intellectually but struggled with in daily living. He was working on turning the past over to Him, but old habits could be hard to break.

Frisky whined and lay his chin on Ian's chest.

"Okay, okay. I'm getting up." He glanced at his bedside clock. It was past eight. He shot to his feet. Lightheadedness cautioned him to move slower. "You should have wakened me earlier, boy. I need to teach you to tell time."

As he walked toward his closet, he rolled his shoulders. His wound protested the movement, but he couldn't let it affect what he needed to get done. He had too much to do.

He dressed in spite of his injury in record time, grabbed an apple and a mug of coffee—the pot had been waiting for him for two hours—then left his house. Out on the deck, he drew in a deep breath of the grass-scented air and made his way toward the barn.

Just outside the old doors, Sarah was speaking with Charlie.

When he approached, they stopped talking and peered at him. He had a feeling he'd been the topic of conversation. "What's up? Did something happen last night and no one bothered to tell me?"

Sarah sent Charlie a look, then smiled at him. "The ranch is fine. Peaceful for a change. The guards reported it was quiet."

Charlie frowned, and Ian turned his attention to the ranch hand.

"What's wrong? Something's going on." Ian narrowed his gaze on the older man.

"Tell him," Charlie muttered.

Ian shifted his full attention to her. "Out with it."

"When I went to my Jeep this morning, someone had slashed my tires. I've already had it towed and repaired." She waved her hand toward her SUV. "See everything is fine."

Fine? If that's what she thought, she was crazy. Because it was his fault her tires had been slashed. He thought of the shooting the previous day, and the lightheadedness from that morning came back until he thought he might have to hold on to something. He stilled and breathed slowly until it passed.

The bullets meant for him could have hit her.

The knife used to slash those tires could have cut her.

All because of him. "I want you off this case."

She lifted her chin. "No chance."

"I'll call the sheriff. I'll make Dan retract

his request. I won't have my attacker substituting you for me."

She didn't flinch once but met his glower with her own fierce one. "Forget it. That guy yesterday shot at both of us, and I'm going to find out who he was."

"Then you need to stay at the ranch. We can park your Jeep in my barn. Since we keep it locked at night, it should be okay in there."

Sarah and Charlie exchanged a glance before she said, "Okay, but I'll sleep in the barn."

"I have a spare bedroom."

"If you want me to stay here, that's my condition."

"Why are you so stubborn? I offer you a warm bed, and you insist on sleeping on the hard ground in the barn?"

"If I stay, it will be in the barn, guarding your horses. Frisky will be with you at the house. You have your gun and guards are patrolling the grounds. You should be fine, but remember this person came after Thunder and your cattle. I want to catch him in the act of sabotaging."

"I have a cot in there that you can use," Charlie said in a quiet voice, his head lowered as his boot scuffed the dirt.

Ian glared at him.

Sarah nodded. "Perfect."

He eyed them both. "Fine. At least you'll be near if you need help." Ian glanced from Charlie to Sarah to Charlie. "What are you two not saying to me?"

His ranch hand stroked his whisker-covered chin. "Sarah stayed last night—"

"Charlie!"

"...in the barn."

Ian crossed his arms. "So someone slit your tires here, at the ranch?" While he'd slept, oblivious. His arm could be on fire with pain, but he would not take another pain pill.

Charlie continued to kick the dirt. "Not exactly."

Ian stepped in front of Sarah, inches from her. "Exactly what went on here?"

"I parked my Jeep on the highway in a cutoff by your gate. I thought I hid it well behind some tall brush, but someone found it. It could just be a coincidence."

"Right." Ian scanned the horizon but saw nothing suspicious. Still... "He's probably watching the ranch, waiting for his next chance to do ... no telling what." Furious and worried at the same time, he took off his cowboy hat and shoved his fingers through his hair. "I don't like this one bit. If anything happened—"

She clasped his good arm. "I appreciate your concern, but I can take care of myself. I'm more worried about you."

"I appreciate your concern, but I can take care of myself." He stalked toward the barn.

Inside, he paused, inhaling and exhaling gulps of air to still his rampaging heartbeat. He balled his hands at his sides and wanted to punch the man responsible for all of this. Instead, he saw a sack of feed nearby and rammed his fist into it, spilling it out on the ground. He didn't care. It felt good to hit something.

Sarah clicked the dishwasher door closed and switched the machine on. She swept around to find Ian lounging against the doorjamb. His eyes softened as they took her in. A warmth flowed through her at his expression. She remembered that look. She'd seen it often, just moments before he'd wrapped her in his arms and kissed her. She wanted to turn away. She wouldn't surrender her heart again. She'd done that once. She didn't think it would survive another break. That was why she insisted on staying in the barn.

Silence hung between them.

"The meal was delicious," he finally said, sauntering toward her. "My idea of fish is fried catfish, but your grilled salmon was great. I might have to expand my food preferences."

Small talk. Like at dinner. She could play that game. "I enjoy cooking. It's a kind of therapy for me. I like coming up with different recipes. If I'm really stressed, I bake. And then I give the treats away."

"Any time you want to do that, I'll take one." He edged into her personal space.

A tingling sensation started in her stomach and spread throughout her body.

The effect of his nearness hadn't changed in all the years of separation. Desperate to keep this as professional as possible, she sidestepped and moved away. "We need to discuss the people on your list. Who've you ruled out? Who's still on it?"

He expelled a long breath. "Sure. Let's go into my office."

She led the way and took her place at one end of the leather couch. Earlier, she'd put her notes on the coffee table, so she grabbed them as Ian sat. "I think we should start with who we can mark off the list then talk through each person still on it."

Frisky wandered in and lay near Ian's feet. He leaned down and scratched the dog. "I worked through my half of the list, checking on each person's whereabouts the last couple of days, and I ruled out all but two."

"Excellent. I have just one on my list. My guy is Jagger Burns. I can't find him anywhere."

"My two are Tim Downs and Larry Pickens. Burns is right up there with them as far as ruthless and dangerous go."

"It's also possible one of these other guys hired someone else to do the dirty work."

He waved his paper in the air. "I don't think so. If they want revenge, they want to be the ones doing it."

"Assuming one of them is the culprit. I know you told your neighbor he'd never receive the land if you die, but nothing happened last night after you talked with him."

He pinned her with a sharp look, a frown on his face. "Have you forgotten your slashed tires? That happened last night. It's because you're investigating this case."

"We don't know if that's related." Although she thought it probably was. It wasn't like she didn't have her own enemies. "It could be the people behind the cattle rustling."

"No cattle have gone missing for a couple of weeks. They may have moved on to greener pastures. If I were a rustler, I wouldn't want to stay too long in any one place."

"Dan and I have been wondering about

that. We're looking at rustling cases all over the Southwest."

Ian stared at his half sheet. "For argument's sake, let's include Taylor. That gives us four suspects."

She sighed. "I can't shake the feeling you're missing someone."

His frown deepened. "I've been thinking that, too."

"You've been retired and home for six months. Think about what happened toward the end of your career. Revenge can fester for years, especially for someone in a jail cell, but it's more likely this is connected to something that happened more recently. Besides your neighbor, is there anyone else in Blue Creek you've hacked off? A ranch hand you let go?"

He stared toward the window and after a moment shook his head. "Dad had cut back and only Charlie and Tony were still working for him. To tell you the truth, I was looking for some extra help, but I hadn't found anyone yet."

"Turn anyone down?"

"I haven't had an interview yet. I've

had a few recommendations, but I'd thoroughly checked each one out first. So far, no one's gotten past that stage. I do have someone I'm going to talk to who I think will be great, but I'm not interviewing him until next week."

Tension clamped around her shoulder and squeezed. "How about in Houston in the past year? It doesn't even have to be related to work." She rubbed her neck and began to move further down.

"Here let me do that."

She hesitated for a few seconds, but the streak of pain spreading down her back prompted her to turn.

He scooted toward her and rubbed her shoulders. "From the last year? Hmm..."

His words seemed far away as she enjoyed the massage.

"Those criminals are in prison or jail awaiting trial."

She forced herself to concentrate. "Anyone associated with them?"

"I don't think so. But I'll talk with my former partner and see what he says."

The feel of his fingers kneading her

muscles began to alleviate the pain. She closed her eyes and relished the relief. "Any case stand out to you?"

His fingers stopped for a moment, then started again. A little more pressure this time. "My last one. It's the reason I quit."

She ducked under his hands and turned. "What happened?"

His gaze darkened, and his hands dropped to his lap. In seconds his expression evolved into one of anguish. "Kidnapping. Doug and Julie Henderson."

"That was a tragedy. I remember reading about some of it on the Internet. I didn't realize—"

"The kidnapper robbed that family of justice. The coward killed himself. Julie's parents fell apart. Her mother was hospitalized and still hasn't really recovered. Last I heard, she was in a mental hospital. Julie was six months pregnant with their first grandchild. The doctors tried to save the baby but..."

His words trailed off, but she could see the anguish on his face. She hadn't known he'd been involved in that case. Now, she could see how it affected him.

"After that ... I couldn't do it anymore. I thought I'd been hardened, but there was something about it that got to me."

Sarah clasped Ian's cold fingers. "It wasn't your fault."

"I was lead on the case. If I'd done something different..." He blew out a long breath. "Maybe she and her child would be alive today. I can't get that out of my mind."

Her heart twisted. She wanted to ease his pain as he had hers. She cradled his face in her palms. "I understand that anguish. I've been there."

He pulled his gaze from the far wall to her eyes. "Tell me."

"Two dead teenagers. They'd been caught up in human trafficking, abused and discarded. I dream about them sometimes. What would their lives have been like if they hadn't been lured into prostitution?"

He covered her hand with his and tugged her against him, his arms entwining around her. She pressed against him, listening to his heartbeat. Its sound gave her a sense she belonged there, in his embrace.

When she lifted her head, she studied his features. He'd hardly changed over the years. Those eyes—an electric blue. That mouth—full and enticing.

Ian leaned slowly toward her, pausing a moment, like he was waiting for permission.

And then he kissed her.

FIVE

Ian's lips grazed across Sarah's as though a faint breeze caressed her. When she didn't tug away but instead inched closer, he deepened the kiss, pouring out all the emotions he'd locked away for fifteen years. The feel of her in his arms sated a need in him, and yet he still yearned for more. Much more.

Finally, he drew back before he took it a step further.

There was no doubt that he was in danger. If he could change their circumstances in order to protect her, he would. But when he'd insisted she go home rather than sit in front of his house in her car, she ignored his wishes. What if she'd surprised the person who slit her tires? She might've been hurt—protecting him. If he could keep her close, he could be sure nobody would hurt her. The thought of having her near gave him peace, and not just because he knew she'd be safer.

He noticed an enticing blush in her cheeks and inched back to his end of the couch. "We'll tell Dan tomorrow the names of the three people we've narrowed the list down to and give him their pictures. That way he and his deputies can be on the lookout for them. The sheriff already knows about Taylor."

She looked down, smoothed her slacks, stared at the floor. "Sounds good. I'll do the same with the sheriffs in the surrounding the counties. Unless it's Taylor—and I agree with you that he seems unlikely—then the person has to be staying somewhere. Maybe we'll get lucky, it'll be one of these three, and someone will ID the culprit." She combed her hair behind her ears and kept her eyes downcast.

"Any report on the forensic evidence?"

She straightened her shoulders and faced him. The blush was gone. "Nothing there. We do know a type of rat poison was used, and I'm looking into sources for buying it in large qualities."

"Doc Miller called me about the poison. Problem is, that stuff could have been added over several days. Plus, the person probably bought it at different places, so he didn't raise suspicion."

"Can it be cleaned up effectively?"

"I'm working with the authorities on doing that." So much had been done already, and so much still needed doing. But here he was, staring as she bit her bottom lip, and all he could think about was how much he wanted to kiss her again. If only they could forget all this, even for a few moments.

But she was pulling away, putting up her professional barrier between them.

"Did you ever run a complete check on Tony?"

He shook his head. "Dad hired him, and he's been working here for five years with no problems. I figure that speaks for him."

She flattened her lips in a hard line. "Hmm. I did some investigating, and there is no one who matches his description named Tony Zoller, at least in a multiple state area."

Ian rubbed at the whiskers on his chin. Tony? After five years, was Tony doing this? He thought back to the various incidents. He'd certainly had the means and opportunity. But... "Why would he do it?"

"I don't know. I can't ignore I can't run a background check on him."

"Well, much as it pains me to admit it, there are a lot of folks who take to ranching because they're trying to escape a former life. Ranch hands aren't always the cream of the crop, and some ranch owners don't always run background checks. Did you try Anthony Zoller?"

"Yeah. Nothing. And as I said, it's a red flag. So, who is he?"

Ian glanced at the clock on his desk. Nearly midnight. "I'll talk to him first thing tomorrow."

Sarah shoved herself to her feet. "Which is my cue to get some rest. Six will be here faster than I want."

Ian rose, wincing at the ache in his shoulder. He refused to massage it in front of her, lest she insist on another pain killer. "Let me change places. You stay in the house. I'll stay in the barn."

"I don't want to be too comfortable. Otherwise, I'll fall into a deep sleep and may miss something."

He opened his mouth to protest, but she held up her hand, her fingers over his lips. "I need to do my job. It's important to me. Okay?"

He pinched his lips together and tried to think of something to change her mind. She wouldn't. He'd seen that resolved look on her face. "Fine. How about you take Frisky?"

"He's here to warn you if anyone comes into the house. I have a stable full of hors-es to do that."

"They aren't watch dogs."

"I know. But when I got up this morn-ing, they started moving around. They'll alert me if anyone comes in."

Frustration churned his gut. All he

wanted to do was protect her, and she was fighting him at every turn. He spied that star on her chest and reminded himself she didn't need his protection. She was a Ranger. He was a rancher. He released a long breath. "May I walk you to the barn?"

"Then I'd have to turn around and walk you back to the house." Her lips spread into a beautiful smile. "We'd be doing that all night long." Sarah gestured to the window. "Watch from there or from the porch."

"You're a tough negotiator."

"I aim to please." She crossed to the hallway.

He started to follow.

She spun around and backpedaled. "On second thought, watch from the window. That way I know you're in for the night."

"Woman, make up your mind."

Her lips twitched like she wanted to say something, but then the look faded. "It's safer for you. That's what's important to me."

She turned, but he snagged her arm and halted her. He stepped closer until they were just inches apart. "Am I important to you?"

"People involved in my cases are always important to me."

His shoulders sagged.

She leaned toward him and kissed him lightly on the cheek. "Yes. I won't deny I care about you."

A lump of emotion lodged in his throat, and he couldn't utter a word as she swung around and walked away.

He watched from the hallway until she opened the front door and slipped out of his house. As he went back in his office to keep an eye on her until she reached the barn, he whistled an upbeat tune. *She cares about me. I'm important to her. It's a start*.

He watched her walk across the yard toward the barn, her hips swaying just enough. She knew he was watching. Was she smiling, too?

Movement to the right caught his eye, and he turned to glimpse Tony emerging from the shadows on the cabin porch into the light, a cigarette in his hand. Relax, O'Leary. She has her gun. Besides, he didn't see Tony doing this after five years working here, but he would talk to him first thing in the morning.

A moment later, Charlie walked across the yard and joined them. He knew he could trust Charlie, and his heartbeat slowed to a regular rhythm.

Sarah studied Tony as he finished his cigarette, dropped it into the dirt, and ground it with the toe of his boot.

"Ian allows you to smoke here?"

"Yep, at the cabin. Not at the barn or out in the field, especially since it's been dry lately." A defensive tone entered Tony's voice. "I've been smoking since I came and not one problem."

Charlie came out on the porch and joined them a few steps away from the cabin. "Any progress on the case."

She looked from Tony to Charlie, wondering exactly who Tony was. She didn't like a mystery. "Yes, we've narrowed down some suspects." Just to see what Tony would do, she added, "We're close to solving this." *If you call on the other side of the world close.*

"Good." Tony stared off into the darkness across the ranch road. "Well, folks, I'm calling it a night. It's been a long day."

"Me, too." Sarah took a couple of steps back. The hairs on her nape stood up. Was someone out there, beyond the other side of the drive? Instinctively she touched her holster on her belt.

"I'll walk with you to the barn." Charlie fell in beside her. "What's wrong?"

She glanced over her shoulder and watched Tony go inside the cabin. "Does he ever talk about life before he came to the ranch?"

Charlie lifted his chin and tapped his forefinger against it. "Nothing I remember. But I can sometimes tune people out when they go on and on."

Sarah laughed. "Thanks for telling me that. I'll try to keep my comments short and to the point."

"Oh, never with a pretty gal." Charlie winked and stopped in front of the barn. "See you tomorrow morning."

Sarah checked the cavernous interior,

making sure no one had come in and hidden. She spied the decidedly uncomfortable cot already in the doorway and groaned. And she volunteered to sleep here. What was she thinking?

As she pulled the blanket over her, she knew exactly what she'd been thinking. She didn't want anything to happen to Ian. He was a good guy even if he did walk away from her years ago. Thinking of the cases he'd worked on only solidified that in her mind. He'd been in law enforcement two years longer than she, and he'd seen a lot in those extra years. She was glad he was back. He'd gone into the FBI to get revenge, but that kind of fuel would only give you strength for so long. Here on the ranch—this was where he belonged.

When she listened to him talk about the young couple's kidnapping, his voice had cracked. Six months later, and it was as fresh in his mind as the day it happened.

A horse neighed. In another stall, she heard the rustling of hay. The animals were settling down. She needed to sleep if she was going to stay on her feet tomorrow.

She closed her eyes and relaxed her body, one part at a time, a trick she'd learned to help her sleep. Soon she was whisked away...

A loud bang. She woke, listened. Heard it again. It sounded like a horse was kicking at the wooden slats of his stall. Thumps and thuds filled her mind, as though multiple drums were being struck. She sat straight up and swung her legs to the floor.

She stared out into the dimly lit area, a gray haze snaking its way from the opposite side of the barn toward the middle. She bolted up, inhaling the scent of smoke. Coughing, she felt her way to the main light switch and flipped it up. The horses along that far wall were ramming against their stall doors.

Sarah hurried toward the front exit, fumbling for the key she'd stuffed in her pocket. When she pulled it free, she stuck it in the lock and it opened. She pushed on the wooden double doors.

They didn't budge.

Locked from the outside?

Repeated barks jerked Ian from a sound sleep. Frisky sat next to his bed, still yelping even after he sat on the edge of the mattress.

"What's wrong?"

Frisky ran to the door and looked back at Ian.

When he rose, his dog hurried out in the hall, continuing to yap. He hurried and dressed, then grabbed his gun on the bedside table and followed Frisky to the front door. His dog scratched to get out, barking.

Fully alert, Ian rushed out onto the porch, his heart beginning to race. In the distance, flames licked up the far side of the barn, black smoke obscuring the security lighting.

Sarah!

He ran toward the fire. Charlie came out of the cabin nearby with Tony following. For a few seconds they stared at the burning structure, then hurried forward.

Ian's lungs ached. He was still fifteen yards away, inhaling the smoke filling the air, when he noticed in the haze a piece of plywood jammed through the door handles and heard the sounds of something crashing against the exit.

Suddenly the barn's double doors burst open, the board splitting in two. Sarah dashed outside and saw him, then pivoted and ran back in.

She's going after the horses.

He pumped his legs faster. "While I open the back doors and get the horses at that end, help Sarah," he yelled at the two hired hands over the sounds of the blaze.

"We will," Charlie called out then disappeared with Tony into the smoke-filled interior.

Ian vaulted over the east paddock's fence and skirted the corner of the structure to unlock the back doors to rescue the animals from both ends. He normally never had all the stalls full so time was of the essence.

He sent up a thank you to the Lord for the key in his jeans' pocket as he shoved it into the lock, turned it, then opened one of the double doors. Smoke bellowed out of the gap, surrounding him and clouding his view. He coughed and used his shirt to cover his mouth. As he hastened toward the other door, a large shape—a guard?—came out of the haze from the west side of the barn. Before Ian could react, something long and solid struck his head. He crumpled to the ground, trying to retain consciousness, but another whack sent him over the edge into darkness.

When Sarah noticed Ian and the two ranch hands coming, she dashed back into the barn to rescue the horses. Sarah found the tack room, pulled the pillowcase off the cot, and felt her way to the sink. After wetting the cloth and tying it around her face, she dove back into the main area to free the animals.

Charlie and Tony passed her, the older man shouting to her, "We'll take this longer row. You the other one."

A gray cloud engulfed her, but through the haze she saw the wall of flames on the west side. Her eyes watered and stung. Crackling sounds of the fire vied with the pounding of hooves and frightened noises of the horses trying to get out of their deathtrap.

Praying the horses found their way out- side, Sarah started to open the few stalls on the west side before the flames totally engulfed that part of the barn. Through the smoke, she barely made out any horses, but their screams overrode the noise from the fire. Even as she breathed through the wet pillowcase, smoke invaded her lungs. She coughed and sputtered and kept going. At the last stall, the wide-eyed mare kicked the wooden half door blocking her escape. Sarah flung it wide, jumping out of the mare's path.

The scared animal charged out, but in- stead of heading toward the front, it came right at Sarah. She scrambled sideways, trying to get out of the way. The horse passed her, clipping her shoulder and knocking her back. She grabbed for some- thing to hold onto, but there was nothing but smoke. She fell, her bottom slamming into the hard dirt, her cloth about her face slipping down around her neck.

She blinked and tried to get her bearings. She scanned the wall of gray, listening to the snapping and popping of the fire as it made its way up the west wall. Coughs racked her, and she pressed the wet pillowcase over her mouth and nose again, then pushed herself to her feet.

The smoke was thicker, and she could hardly see. Which way was out? She fell to her knees and searched the gray and flames for freedom.

The back doors flung open. Now she knew which direction she could go. She pushed her way forward, keeping low but still inhaling a lungful of smoke on her way. A few feet from the rear door, she stumbled over something. She reached down and felt the soft cotton of a shirt.

A horse flew by Sarah as she grabbed the man's legs and dragged him toward the opening. Out of the smoke another large beast barreled toward her. She dropped the man's feet and lay on top of his jean-clad legs as the horse leaped over her.

Hurrying, she scrambled up, and with her adrenaline-fueled strength, hauled him the remaining few feet to the exit and beyond. Outside in the clearer air and the light from the fire, she got a good look at the man she'd brought out of the barn.

Ian! She bent over him, her chest burning. Coughing.

There were men there. She glimpsed three or four, and she didn't recognize them. She reached for her gun and then realized—guards, of course. Two of them lifted Ian's limp body and carried him further from the blaze. After she'd inhaled a few good breaths, she swiveled and followed them. *Please let him be okay*. Then she looked at the men and thought, *please let them really be guards*.

She had no idea how Ian had ended up knocked out inside. Had a panicked horse run him down?

As the men placed Ian on the grass-covered ground, he stirred. She pushed aside one of the guards and knelt next to him. The heat from the blaze caused sweat to roll down her face.

She swiped her hand across her forehead and assessed the wound on the side of his head. *What in the world?* "Has any-one called 911?" The question came out in a hoarse whisper. The man closest to her crunched his brow as if he hadn't heard her. She tugged him closer. "Call 911. He needs an ambulance."

"Yes, ma'am." The guard rose and pulled out his cell phone.

Ian reached out and touched her hand. "I'm okay, Sarah." His voice was raspy and weak.

"No, you're not. No argument." She ended the last word with a bout of cough-ing.

"Look who's talking." One corner of Ian's mouth lifted for a few seconds. "You're safe. Thank God." And then he passed out.

After being treated for mild smoke inhala-tion in the ER, Sarah prowled around Ian's hospital room, checking her watch every few seconds. He'd stay in overnight for ob-servation for his concussion and smoke in-halation—as soon as he got here. She hadn't seen him since the paramedics transported them in separate ambulances hours before.

Charlie came in. "Where's our patient?"

She blew out a long breath. "They said he was getting a CT scan. How long can one take? I need to see him." She continued the pacing and watch-checking.

"Settle down, Sarah." Charlie sat on the couch, exhaustion lining his face. "You're making me tired. You told me on the phone the doctors said he'd been awake and alert, right?"

Sarah nodded. "They've been running a series of tests on him for both the concussion and the smoke inhalation, but he's tough. He'll be good as new in a couple of days." She prayed. "Thanks for bringing my Jeep. When's Tony coming to pick you up?"

"Not until I call him."

She sighed and leaned against the empty bed. "So, how bad is it?"

"The barn is gone, but the fire department managed to keep the fire from spreading beyond that. Worse part—a horse died. A pregnant mare."

Sarah gripped the bar on one side of the bed, her eyelids sliding down as she thought of how this news would affect Ian.

"He's got good insurance, but some losses are hard to replace."

"Like Thunder."

"Yes, child. Everything is being done to recover him, but who knows?" The older man's shoulders slumped. "Especially if the thief keeps him holed up somewhere."

"If we find the person doing this ... Was Tony with you the whole time?"

"You really do suspect him."

"No more than the others we're investigating on the list. What disturbs me is the culprit might not be on the list." Finally Sarah plopped onto the chair next to the small couch. "If I hadn't stumbled over Ian, he could have died in that fire." Her voice quavered, and she hugged her arms across her chest, trying her best to compose herself. Ian hadn't died.

Thank You, Lord, but what happens next time? He's escaped twice. How many more chances would Ian get?

"You still love him."

She wanted to deny it, but she couldn't. When he'd left her, she'd shut herself off from the world. Sure, she'd dated, but her relationships had been casual, not much more than friends really. "What makes you think that?"

"You have that same look you did fifteen years ago. He's not the same boy who left here intent on revenge."

"I know, but that presents its own set of doubts."

"Follow your heart."

"You never answered my question about Tony."

Charlie stroked his chin. "Well, we both were sleeping, so I can't rightly tell you. I'm a light sleeper. I didn't hear him leaving. When I smelled smoke, he was in his bed sleeping." He shrugged. "So you be the judge."

"Truthfully, I don't think it was him, because he was busy rescuing the horses when someone attacked Ian."

"Yep, so see you've been able to scratch one person off that list."

She started to reply when the door

opened and an orderly wheeled Ian into the room. He saw her and his face lit up with a smile that reached deep into his eyes.

"I thought I might have imagined you at the fire. I've been asking about you, but no one told me much. You okay?"

"Better than you. The doc isn't keeping me overnight." She returned his grin, suddenly feeling much better now that she had seen him.

Ian rose from the wheelchair and took several steps to the bed. Once he was settled on it, the orderly left. "I think the staff conspired to keep us apart. I've wanted to tell you something all day."

"What?" She came to the side of his bed, wondering what he and Charlie would do if she leaned over and kissed him.

"I think I know who's doing this."

Ian's words jerked Sarah from her thoughts. "You think? Who?"

"Not his name, but I've been thinking while waiting for all the tests to be run. I remember someone leaning over me with his hair graying at his temples. He had a big nose, kinda crooked, like maybe it had been broken at one time. I think."

"But you're not sure?" Sarah brushed a dark lock from Ian's forehead.

"When I try too hard to think too much, my headache pounds even more. Some of the facial features are there, just out of focus."

"Don't force it. You have a concussion. At least you have some memory of the guy. I don't recall any of the men left on our list having graying hair or a big nose. Maybe it was recently broken and therefore swollen. Prison can certainly age a few men." She couldn't shake this nagging feeling it was someone they hadn't considered yet. "Do we have the most recent photos of the suspects?"

"Just their prison photos."

"Tomorrow, I'll see what I can get that's more recent."

"Charlie." Ian started to sit forward but winced and stayed where he was. "Give me the bad news. I know the barn couldn't have survived the fire. Did we lose any horses?"

The older man came to the bed. "It's a

good thing we live near town. The firefighters contained it. But we lost My Fair Lady."

Ian slid his eyes closed and released a rush of air that sent him into a spasm of coughing. "Thunder sired My Fair Lady's foal." he finally said when he'd calmed down and was breathing normally. "We're going to find this person and make him pay for what he did."

Charlie struck his fist into his palm. "I'm looking forward to teaching him a few lessons."

Ian nodded. "Right now I need you at the ranch. Call the security agency and add some more guards, a few in the daytime, too. I'll be home tomorrow. In the meantime, once the fire chief says we can, I want to start cleaning up the barn rubble. Are all the horses in the pasture again?"

Charlie nodded. "I'll use those extra guards to stay on them twenty-four seven."

"Good. Make sure the guards are on the lookout for a grass fire. I could see him trying that next. This guy isn't going to win."

Charlie plucked his cowboy hat off the small couch. He donned it, tipped the brim at Sarah, then left.

"I don't know what I would have done without Charlie after Dad passed away." Ian closed his eyes. "I feel like a bucking bronco tossed me and stomped on me."

"Rest. I'm staying the night. I don't want this guy coming to finish you off. He's been toying with you. Going after things that mean something to you. That is until tonight. He left you to die in the fire."

"Yeah, I know. I've tried to think of someone who wants me to suffer like this. Most of the criminals are pretty straightforward. They would find me and shoot me. End of story." He covered her hand on the bed. "I don't want you to stay. You need your rest, too."

"I'm going to get some." She pointed to the small couch. "Right there. But not until you go to sleep."

"Are you bribing me?"

"Me?" She smiled. "Maybe. Is it going to work?"

His mouth quirked, but he didn't maintain the grin as he shut his eyes. A few moments later, his head lolled to the side.

She bent forward and kissed his cheek, praying the Lord would keep him safe. *Ian is in Your hands, God*.

"I can't believe they want to run more tests. I just want to get out of here." Ian grumbled the next morning in his hospital room.

Sarah sat in an uncomfortable chair close to his bed and stretched the kinks out of her sore body. Who knew the couch could be worse than that cot in the barn? "They're just making sure you're okay before they release you."

"All they had to do was ask. I'd have told them I'm fine." He scooted to the side of the bed, his legs dangling over the edge.

"That's the problem. You'd say anything to get out of here."

"Can you blame me? I don't care what Charlie says. My whole ranch could've gone up in flames, and he'd have said it was fine, just to make sure I stayed here."

The door swung open, and an orderly entered the room pushing a wheelchair.

"You ready?"

Sarah stood and stretched again. "I'm heading to the ranch. I'll get you some clothes and shoes to wear home. The ones you came in are trashed."

"I could always wear this lovely hospital gown." He chuckled and sat in the wheelchair.

Sarah walked out with Ian and the orderly and rode the elevator to the first floor. After the orderly rolled Ian through double doors for his tests, she headed into the sunny day. Twenty minutes later, Sarah drove through the gates of the ranch.

That empty space where the barn used to be drew her attention. She parked in front of it and stared. She could still smell its remains, and she scrunched up her nose against the memories. She stepped out of her car and remembered the terror of the night before. Something blocking the double doors so they didn't open. The sounds of the panicked horses in their stalls behind her. The absolute certainty that she would die, her hopeless prayer that the smoke would take her before the flames licked at her heels.

But she'd survived.

A crowd of folks were working to clear the debris, Charlie and Tony among them. Some guards stood around the perimeter while the horses grazed as if nothing had happened. The sun warmed the spring air, but the sight of that barn reminded her there was a killer on the loose. No doubt about it now, because if she hadn't tripped over Ian, he'd be dead. After she brought Ian home, she would throw herself into the case and find the assailant.

The thought hurried Sarah's footsteps toward the house. She'd grab some clothes and boots for Ian then return to the hospital. She wanted to be there when Ian was finished with his tests.

She unlocked the front door with the key Charlie had given her yesterday and stepped into the quiet house. She'd have expected Frisky to greet her, but then she remembered he'd been outside with Ian when he'd come toward the burning barn. The dog was probably bunking down with Charlie and Tony.

So many memories besieged her as she walked toward Ian's bedroom to get some clothes. Most were happy ones, but even the bad times didn't really mean anything. Not now, after she'd almost lost him. She loved him, and even their time apart hadn't changed that. She'd been trying to protect her heart since seeing him again. What a waste of time. She'd given it to him years ago.

When she stepped into his bedroom, she froze. A chill swept through her. Everything had been destroyed, torn to shreds, or shattered. Fingers on the handle of her gun, she whirled to check the rest of the house.

In the doorway stood an older man with graying hair and a large bulbous nose. He held a revolver trained on her.

SIX

With a headache still hammering against his skull, Ian paced his hospital room. Where was Sarah? She should have been back by now. He'd tried calling her, but it had gone to voicemail. It wasn't like her not to answer.

He tried Charlie. "Is Sarah there?"

"Yep. She's been up at the house for a while. Is something wrong?"

Relieved nothing happened to her on the way, Ian stopped near his bed. "She was supposed to get some clothes and shoes for me and be right back. That was over an hour ago. Can you go check on her and call me? She isn't answering her cell."

"Sure."

A niggling in the back of Ian's mind took hold and grew as he continued to prowl the room, too restless to sit and wait. He'd had another nightmare about the Hendersons. Why had he been dreaming about them so much lately? When he'd first come to the ranch, the nightmares had faded.

He stopped. Julie Henderson's father, Robert Carter. He had graying hair around his face and a big nose. And he'd blamed the FBI for his daughter's murder. Ian had tried to comfort the man, tried to convince him there'd been nothing they could have done to stop that killer. But Carter hadn't been convinced. Ian still remembered his clenched fists and cold stare.

When the phone rang on the bedside table, he snatched up the receiver. "Charlie?"

"Yeah."

That one word reply, and Ian knew something was wrong. "Tell me she's okay?"

A slow exhale. "When I stepped on the porch, a man called out from inside the house. He's got her and said that he was holding Sarah hostage. That if I or anyone else came closer, he'd kill her."

Ian sank onto the bed, trying to assimilate the situation while his head throbbed. My fault. All my fault. "I'm on my way. Stay away from the house, and make sure everyone else does, too."

After he disconnected with Charlie, Ian immediately placed a call to Dan and explained the situation, as though he were an FBI agent again and the hostage wasn't a woman he loved. He had to be professional, shut down his emotions and come up with a way to save Sarah.

She would not die because of him.

But Robert Carter was out for revenge, and how better to get back at Ian for his failure to save his daughter and unborn grandchild than to kill the woman he loved?

Sarah sat on the couch in Ian's office and watched her captor. He stood against the wall away from the windows, blinds drawn. Dark circles ringed his eyes. His skin was sallow and sickly. He kept his gun aimed at her chest while hers was stuffed in his pocket.

"Who are you? Why are you doing this?"

"Ian O'Leary will know when he finds us."

"*Finds us?*"

"When he comes, I'm going to make him suffer."

She mentally flipped through the photos of all the people who might have a grudge against Ian. She couldn't remember seeing this man's picture. "Tell me about your suffering. Were you in prison?"

He cackled, almost hysterically. "I guess you could call it a prison. He took away everyone I loved, and he's gonna find out what that feels like. I could've just killed him, I suppose. Thought about it. Tried it a couple of times. But that would be too easy."

"Why me? I'm on the case of his missing stallion."

"Sure you are. And why would a Texas Ranger be concerned about a stolen horse? Then I did some checking, and when I watched you two, my suspicions were confirmed. Y'all are in love."

She shook her head vehemently. "No, no. We were once, a long time ago, but we went our separate ways. I'm working the case because the sheriff thought it might be connected to the cattle rustling in the area."

"Sure, lady. I've seen him with you. He loves you. That's all that matters to me."

That sudden sense of loss was so profound, her heart seemed to collapse. They'd been so close. She'd lost him when one madman had bombed the federal building. And now he'd lose her because of another madman out for revenge. How would Ian live with it?

No. She would survive this. They would have their second chance.

Her hands were tied, but her feet were free. She might be able to do...something.

But what? Her captor hadn't taken his eyes off her since she'd sat on the couch. Maybe a distraction outside would give her time to run for the front door. Maybe she could rush him, overtake him. Maybe...

One plan after another tumbled through her thoughts, but when she played them out, in each one, she ended up dead.

Arrive at the ranch, tell Carter he's there, negotiate her release.

That's what the book said.

But if the man was reenacting how his daughter had been killed, then that would be the cue Carter was waiting for to kill her.

Ian had come up with a better plan, one that had a chance, however slight, of saving her life.

He hid in a grove of trees and looked through Dan's binoculars at the area around the cellar opening. The small bulkhead was tucked on the side of the house, away from the barn and the viewing eyes of the crowd that had gathered out front. Charlie, Tony, guards and cops everywhere. Watching the front door. More police officers were keeping an eye on the back door.

And there, on the side of the house, was the bulkhead. It was covered by holly bushes his mother had planted years ago.

His father had rarely pruned them. Unless a person was searching for it, he wouldn't see it.

"Are you sure about this?" Dan pushed a branch aside and squinted across the field.

"This is her only chance. If we rush the place, he'll kill her. If we negotiate, he'll kill her. That's his plan. He's just waiting for me to show up so I can hear the gunshots."

"After what you told me on the phone, I did some checking. His wife died last week. She was in some mental hospital."

He nodded. "So that's what set him off. I hope no one else has to die because of what happened. And that includes Robert."

"That might have set him off, but what he's done in a short time reflects planning. I don't think he could've thrown all this to-gether in less than a week, especially when you figure the amount of rat poison he used in that pond."

Ian frowned, his grasp on the binoculars tightening. "He was waiting for his wife to die. I know she tried to kill herself not long after Julie was killed."

Dan took the binoculars. "I'm going to say this, but I know you're going to ignore my advice. You just got out of the hospital. I should be going in there. Not you."

Ian clasped his friend's shoulder. "I appreciate the offer, Dan, but I'm the only one who can do this. This is between Robert and me." His headache and other pains were nothing compared to what he would feel if something happened to Sarah.

"What do you want us to do?"

"Nothing until I give you the all clear sign."

"What if I hear gunshots?"

"Then I failed, and you'll have to clean up my mess."

Ian studied the one window on the east side of the house. "It looks like he closed all the blinds. I can't tell where he is, but with the blinds closed, at least I should be able to get to the cellar undetected." He checked his weapon one last time, slipped it into the holster, and nodded to Dan. "Wish me luck."

"I'll go one better. I'll pray."

"Robert Carter needs those prayers,

too."

Carrying bolt cutters and a flashlight, Ian crouched and ran toward the holly bushes that disguised the entrance behind the brush. These doors hadn't been used in thirty years. In fact, the cellar had only been used when there was a tornado warning. It was dark and dank, and his mother had hated it.

He crawled between two bushes, found the lock, and cut through the metal. The doors rested at a sixty-degree slant, and when he tried to lift one of them, he couldn't swing it wide because of the brush that had grown up around the entrance. He managed to squeeze through a gap and ease the door back in place quietly. A musky odor assailed his nostrils. He switched on his flashlight, descended the six steps, and surveyed the cellar. Empty but for cobwebs and dust. He hurried across to the stairs and crept up.

His heartbeat thundered in his head, making it throb. He waited until the feeling passed and inhaled a composing breath. *Lord, please help me. I can't do this with-*

out You.

He inched the door open. When it was wide enough, he poked his head out and checked up and down the hallway. He crept out of the cellar and paused to listen.

"We've been friends for years, but that's all it is." Sarah's voice, strong. Pleading. Coming from further down the hall.

"Maybe on your part. Not his. And that's what matters to me," Robert said, and Ian recognized that deep voice, remembered the anguish he'd heard in it, so many times.

They were in the office. Ian pictured the room's floor plan. Robert wouldn't be near a window, even if the blinds were closed. Ian turned and set the flashlight and bolt cutters on the basement steps and drew his gun. After another calming breath, he crept down the hallway, praying he didn't step on any squeaky boards.

"We're like brother and sister," Sarah said. "Ian is in the hospital. He's in bad shape. You nearly killed him."

"I'm glad he lived. This will be better. He'll know what my life has been like these past months."

"He won't come. He's too weak. So, if that is what you think will happen, you're going to be disappointed." Sarah's voice held a strength that amazed Ian.

"Stop lying to me! We'll wait until he gets here." Robert was unraveling, and all of Sarah's pleading and logic weren't doing any good.

At the doorway, Ian flattened himself against the wall and peeked into the room. Sarah sat on the couch across from the door, but Ian couldn't see Robert.

Sarah caught sight of him, blinked, and returned her attention to a spot behind the open door. "I need to go to the restroom."

"Tough," the older man said.

"I haven't done anything to you. We're obviously going to be here for a while. The bathroom down the hall doesn't have any windows, so there's no way I can escape. Besides, you've got both guns."

"No."

Sarah rose from the couch. "Do you think your daughter would approve of what you're doing?"

Ian's heart stalled. He stood outside and willed her to sit down.

"Leave Julie out of this," Robert yelled.

"Would your wife approve?"

Robert stormed into Ian's view, waving the gun, fury exhibited in every line of his body. "Sit down."

"I'm the one you want, Robert." Ian lifted his Magnum 45 and aimed it at Robert's back.

The older man whirled around and fired. The bullet hit the doorframe. Sarah rammed into Robert, knocking him back. His weapon flew out of his hand. He and Sarah both collapsed. She rolled off of him, and Ian rushed forward and pinned him down.

He yanked his handcuffs out of his back pocket and looked at Sarah, crumpled against his wall. "Are you all right? Did he hurt you?" He rolled Robert over and handcuffed him.

"I'm all right. What took you so long?"

Her lighthearted tone set his heart beating again. He sighed. "I s'pose I could've shown up in a hospital gown."

Grinning, he looked toward her. She was the most beautiful sight he'd ever seen. Then his smile faded. "What were you trying to do, get yourself killed?"

"Figured I was dead anyway, if you didn't show up. He wasn't planning to negotiate anything but his own death—and mine. What did I have to lose? He was going to kill me then himself when you came."

"I realized that." He closed his eyes and thought of all the other ways it could've turned out. He grasped both of Robert's arms and jerked him to his feet. "You get the pleasure of arresting him. He'll have a lot of years in prison to think about what he's done."

Sarah held up her hands for Ian to untie. While he did, she read Robert his rights.

Two days later, Sarah sat in the sheriff's office, wrapping up the case against Robert Carter. "I hope the man can get some help. The deaths of his daughter and wife sent him over the edge."

"No excuse for what he did." Dan sat back in his chair.

"I agree, especially since I was the one he held hostage."

"Ian told me your concerns about Tony's hidden past. I had a chat with the cowhand. He had some crazy lady stalking him, so he changed his name and moved halfway across the country. I quietly checked his story, and it's true."

Sarah shifted in her chair. "That's what I hate about our job—having to suspect everyone until proven otherwise. I'm glad he didn't do it."

"Have you seen Ian lately?"

"Not much since I arrested Robert. I had a lot of paperwork to do. Then I slept for a couple of days, and—"

"In other words, you're avoiding him."

"You and I have been friends for a long time. You know me well. Ian nearly got himself killed several times. He left me once. I could have lost—"

"You're scared, Sarah. You love him, and you're afraid of what that could mean."

She put her hands on the arms of the

chair and pushed up. "Since when have you started an advice column?"

"I've known you both since childhood, so you'll get my friendly advice. Go see him. He's been keeping himself busy with the ranch, but you two need to hash this out."

Her cell phone buzzed, indicating a text message. Sarah looked at the screen.

Help. My heart is broken. Can you fix it?

She chuckled. "I'm needed at the Shamrock Ranch."

Half an hour later, she pulled up to the area where the barn had once stood. The charred ruins had been cleared away, and stacks of new lumber sat nearby, waiting for the rebuilding of the barn.

The past couple of days, she had purposely kept it all business with Ian, even to the point of using the case's wrap up as an excuse not to see him. She wanted to be sure how she felt before they had a heart to heart.

She climbed out of her car and approached him. He was leaning forward against a paddock, watching a beautiful black horse trot across the field. "Is that Thunder?"

Ian turned and rested against the wooden slats, a smile on his face, a twinkle in his eyes. "Yes, thanks to you getting the information from Robert, I was able to track down the guy Robert sold him to, and the police in Arizona found him. He arrived this morning, and the vet just left. Thunder is in good condition in spite of his ordeal."

"Oh." She gave him a mocking frown. "I thought you needed me to fix your heart because you couldn't get Thunder back."

He pushed his cowboy hat up on his forehead and seized her gaze while he drew her to him, roping her against him with his arms. "Nope, but now that life is returning to normal, we need to talk."

"About your broken heart?"

"Yep. What are you going to do about it? You're the reason it's broken."

Nestled against him, she tilted her head, and for a full minute, pondered the question she already knew the answer to. "Mmm. I don't know. What do you suggest?"

He burst out laughing. "That's all you can come up with?"

"I've been busy. First, I solved this case, then I nursed my man back to health, and to top all that off, in case you forgot, I was held as a hostage. What do you expect from me?"

He hiked up both of his eyebrows. "I'm your man?"

"I wouldn't do all that just for anyone. I love you, Ian. That hasn't changed since we were teenagers."

He tightened his embrace, lifting her off the ground and swinging her around. "I love you, Sarah. That hasn't changed since we were teenagers. So what I expect from you is a yes to my marriage proposal. We've waited long enough."

Her face radiated with a smile. "I could point out *not because of me*, but I won't. Yes, I'll marry you."

"Good. Now I don't have to hold you hostage until you agreed." He lowered her feet to the ground, then cupped her face in his large hands. "Let's seal our pledge with a kiss."

She brought his head down and pressed her lips into his and put all the love she felt in that kiss.

Dear Reader,

Thank you for reading *Deadly Intent*, the second book in the **Strong Women, Extraordinary Situations Series**. The first book in the series is *Deadly Hunt*. The third book is called *Deadly Holiday*, highlighting another strong woman (a single mom and teacher) faced with dangerous circumstances. The fourth is *Deadly Countdown,* and the fifth, *Deadly Noel.*

Margaret Daley

Check out other books by Margaret Daley at http://margaretdaley.com/all-books/

DEADLY HOLIDAY

Book 3 in
Strong Women, Extraordinary Situations
by Margaret Daley

Tory Caldwell witnesses a hit-and-run, but when the dead victim disappears from the scene, police doubt a crime has been committed. Tory is threatened when she keeps insisting she saw a man killed and the only one who believes her is her neighbor, Jordan Steele. Together, can they solve the mystery of the disappearing body and stay alive?

Excerpt from
DEADLY HOLIDAY
Book 3

Tory Caldwell released a long breath. Ah, a weekend to do nothing but relax and rest. *The best gift I could have right now after the past four months. If only that were possible...*

After dropping her ten-year-old son Morgan off to spend the weekend with his best friend, Tory headed down the mountain toward Crystal Creek, a little town nestled at the bottom of a mountain in the Colorado Rockies. Although mid-December, the next few days were supposed to be above freezing with no chance of snow, so Morgan had pleaded with her to let him stay with Josh, who lived at nine thousand feet.

As she navigated the curvy two-lane road, she mentally ticked off her long list of chores and Christmas shopping to be completed before she returned to school on Monday.

Four-thirty Friday afternoon, and it was already starting to get dark. She didn't like to drive this highway at night. Glancing out her rearview mirror, she glimpsed a black sports car speeding around the curve and coming right toward her, at least fifteen miles over the speed limit. When it was practically on her bumper, she noticed the driver's irritated face. All of sudden, the young, blond headed man, no more than twenty, gunned his vehicle and passed her at the start of the most twisty part of the highway.

Tory gasped, gripping the steering wheel.

The reckless driver zipped in front of her, nearly clipping her bumper. She'd barely registered the car's license plate—HOTSHOT—when it disappeared around the bottom of the S-curve. She breathed easier, knowing at least she didn't have to worry about him riding her tail.

When she hit a straight stretch of the road, she spied the black sports car a hundred yards or so ahead. It was veering toward the drop-off on the right side of the highway. The driver swerved, overcompensated and bounded into the other lane—right toward an older gentleman walking on the shoulder next to the mountain.

The car hit the pedestrian. The man flew into the air.

"No!" Tory screamed.

The older man struck the pavement, his body bouncing.

Stunned, Tory slammed on her brakes and skidded several feet while the driver of the sports car slowed for a few seconds, then revved his engine and sped away.

Tory guided her Jeep to the shoulder, parked, then climbed out, shaking so badly that she held her door until she was steady enough to move. A chilly wind cut through her as she crossed to the man lying face up in a pool of blood. He stared up at her with lifeless eyes.

She knelt, and with a trembling hand, she felt for a pulse at the side of his neck. Nothing. She tried again. Still no pulse. Then she hovered her fingertips over his slightly open mouth. No breath. She wished she knew CPR, but from the looks of him she didn't think it would have mattered.

She straightened and scanned the area. Deserted. Except for the black sports car, she hadn't seen any other vehicles since she'd started back to Crystal Creek. Not a lot of people lived on the top of this side of the mountain.

As she took one final sweep of her surroundings, she spied a wallet and set of keys not far from the older gentleman. She picked up the brown billfold and flipped it open to see if there was any identification. A photo of a man who looked like the one on the pavement declared the victim was Charles Nelson, seventy-two years old. The address indicated he lived nearby. He had probably been on his way home. Since this was a crime scene, she returned the wallet to where she found it. She shouldn't have touched it in the first place, but at least she could tell the 911 operator who the victim was.

Shivering, she dug into her coat pocket and removed her phone, praying she had driven far enough toward the main highway to get cell reception. No bars. Dead as the man at her feet.

She could return to Josh's house, but she knew a gas station/grocery store was closer down the mountain. If there wasn't cell reception, the place would have a land-line phone she could use. Not wanting to involve her son in this, she chose to contin-ue toward the highway.

Ten minutes later, she sat in the store's parking lot and punched in 911 on her cell phone. After she reported the hit-and-run, she took a few minutes to compose herself. Her hands were still shaking. She'd never seen a wreck like that. Then she went in-side to use the restroom, grab something hot to drink, and then head back up the mountain to wait for the police. When she arrived at the spot of the hit-and-run thirty minutes later, all she found was the blood on the pavement. The body was gone.

DEADLY HUNT

Book 1 in
Strong Women, Extraordinary Situations
by Margaret Daley

All bodyguard Tess Miller wants is a vacation. But when a wounded stranger stumbles into her isolated cabin in the Arizona mountains, Tess becomes his lifeline. When Shane Burkhart opens his eyes, all he can focus on is his guardian angel leaning over him. And in the days to come he will need a guardian angel while being hunted by someone who wants him dead.

DEADLY COUNTDOWN

Book 4 in
Strong Women, Extraordinary Situations
by Margaret Daley

Allie Martin, a widow, has a secret protector who manipulates her life without anyone knowing until...

When Remy Broussard, an injured police officer, returns to Port David, Louisiana to visit before his medical leave is over, he discovers his childhood friend, Allie Martin, is being stalked. As Remy protects Allie and tries to find her stalker, they realize their feelings go beyond friendship.

When the stalker is found, they begin to explore the deeper feelings they have for each other, only to have a more sinister threat come between them. Will Allie be able to save Remy before he dies at the hand of a maniac?

DEADLY NOEL

Book 5 in
Strong Women, Extraordinary Situations
by Margaret Daley

District attorney, Kira Davis, convicted the wrong man—Gabriel Michaels, a single dad with a young daughter. When new evidence was brought forth, his conviction was over-turned, and Gabriel returned home to his ranch to put his life back together. Although Gabriel is free, the murderer of his wife is still out there and resumes killing women. In a desperate alliance, Kira and Gabriel join forces to find the true identity of the person terrorizing their town. Will they be able to forgive the past and find the killer before it's too late?

About the Author

Bestselling author, Margaret Daley, is multi-published with over 90 titles and 5 million books sold worldwide. She had written for Harlequin, Abingdon, Kensington, Dell, and Simon and Schuster. She has won multiple awards, including the prestigious Carol Award, Holt Medallion and Inspirational Readers' Choice Contest.

She has been married for over forty years and has one son and four granddaughters. When she isn't traveling, she's writing love stories, often with a suspense thread and corralling her three cats that think they rule her household.

To find out more about Margaret visit her website at *http://www.margaretdaley.com*.

Made in the USA
Monee, IL
17 May 2021

68744618R00080